The Toast of New Year's Eve

A Newfound Lake Cozy Mystery
Book 8

Virginia K. Bennett

To the members of the writing community who supported me early on, thank you!

Skye Jones
Marissa Farrar
Dawn Edwards
Kat Reads Romance
Kathryn LeBlanc
TL Swan
VR Tennent
Gina Sturino
Rachelle Kampen
...and so many more!

Table of Contents

1. The Before   1
2. The During   10
3. The After   19
4. The Scramble   28
5. The Target   37
6. The Suspect(s)   46
7. The Names   56
8. The Morning   65
9. The Assumption   74
10. The Alias   84

Also by Virginia K. Bennett   95
Recipe   97
About the Author   99

Chapter 1

The Before

"Welcome. Welcome, sweetie. Now, don't you make that outfit look amazing." Rebecca welcomed children of all ages to the New Year's at Noon party. Though it was geared toward kids who wouldn't be staying up until midnight, she didn't discriminate. If a fifteen-year-old signed up, she'd welcome them with open arms. "I hope you all brought your dancing shoes!" she announced.

The amazing team of librarians had, yet again, put together a line-up of activities to entertain the children from around Newfound Lake. Though New Year's Eve fell on a Sunday this year, and the library was typically closed on Sundays, she opened for this special event, knowing they would be closed on Monday for New Year's Day.

Rebecca looked around at the kids then checked her list again. "Jeremy, have you seen Melanie and Megan yet? I thought Heather was dropping them off." Heather

1

was the mother to Melanie and Megan, and also her boyfriend's ex-wife. The divorced pair worked tirelessly to make sure their girls came first even when they could no longer live together. Rebecca was now part of that blended family.

"I haven't, but I'll bring them in if you've already started dancing."

"Thanks. She's taking the girls tonight so Kenny and I can go out for our first New Year's Eve together."

Jeremy smiled. "That was a kind gesture. Guess you guys really have got it all figured out, this co-parenting thing."

"I wouldn't say that, exactly." She held out her hand, palm down, and rotated each side up and down. "We haven't had a single date alone this month. Mind you, it's not all her fault. His work schedule has been crazy. Two officers took other jobs in town, so he's filling in gaps left and right. On the one rare occasion he asked her to help out, just for a single night, she said no. It was a bummer."

Rebecca's red hair fell over her shoulders when she looked down at her shiny flats and smoothed her shimmering skirt. The black sweater she paired with it was covered in a square of gold sequins where she could rub them back and forth between reading 'New Year's Eve' and 'Happy New Year' when the clock struck noon.

"Let's get this party started," encouraged Mary, the octogenarian who showed up practically dressed as the ball from Time's Square.

"Where did you get that jacket?" asked Rebecca, noticing her co-worker's outfit for the first time.

"Thrift store. When you need something to wear one time, it's the best deal. Had to hem up the sleeves just a skosh, but it fit pretty well. Only cost five dollars." She popped the collar on her way to the multi-purpose room with a little pep in her orthopedic step.

"I guess I better get going. Make sure parents sign in any other children that show up," she instructed Jeremy.

"Yes, ma'am." He stood, feet together and back straight, at the door with a clipboard and pen at the ready.

When she entered the multi-purpose room, she turned on a playlist she had prepared earlier in the week. "Are we ready to get to some dancing?" she called out to a room full of children. They responded with hoots and hollers. "The ball drops in two hours." She pointed to a disco ball hanging from the ceiling. "There's no time to waste. Line up so we can learn some fun dances."

She started with the Electric Slide, which proved to be much harder than expected. Her audience was all under ten, so that added to the level of difficulty. Melanie and Megan joined in matching rose gold dresses before she started the second dance, the Cupid Shuffle. This one should have been first, but the Electric Slide just had a nostalgic quality for her.

"Let's all get a drink of punch or water, and then join me back on the floor for some more dancing." Rebecca needed a break, and they had only been going for about ten minutes. This didn't bode well for the rest of the event. Mary had poured cups and arranged them on tables along one wall to speed up the process.

Suddenly, a flash of light came from the entrance to the multi-purpose room. Jeremy had entered with a camera and must have decided it was a good time to take some candid photos.

"Jeremy, why would you take pictures of us getting drinks?"

"I'm learning how to use a real camera, so I didn't know if the lighting was right for the room."

"If you check that photo, I'm guessing a few of these kids will just be giant balls of light due to the sequins." Rebecca waited while he checked. "Was I right?"

"Next time I'll try without the flash." Head down, Jeremy walked over to a chair near the entrance and sat.

Rebecca called the children over again with promises of a new dance. This time, Mary pressed play and the Hokey Pokey started up. Voices cheered for the familiar tune, and everyone sang along while showing off their ability to follow the directions. Again, Rebecca realized this would have been a better first choice.

After they had tried some square dance moves and finished with YMCA, it was time for another drink and a snack the kids could make. All of the possible ingredients for a holiday trail mix were placed in bowls with scoops so each child could customize theirs. Rebecca had asked about allergies when parents signed their kids up and, by sheer luck, there were no kids allergic to nuts. The table offered several types of nuts as well as cereals, pretzels and candies. The trail mix was just as much a snack as it was an activity.

"Children, we're ready to make party poppers." Mary

took the kids over to a different table with dozens of recycled toilet paper tubes and colored tissue paper. With the help of Rebecca and Jeremy to complete some of the necessary twisting and taping, each partygoer was able to construct two tubes filled with wrapped candies and confetti. If they wanted to take them home after the event, they could, but Rebecca predicted a huge mess to clean up when they left. While the party poppers were great fun for the kids, she was happy they didn't make a loud noise the way Christmas crackers did.

Rebecca checked in with Melanie and Megan to make sure they were having fun, but they really didn't need her. Each girl had a close friend from school sign up, so they were having a blast.

When the craft was complete and kids had labeled their work, Jeremy took them back to the middle of the room to play a variety of balloon games. Some games were played in small groups, trying to keep balloons in the air, and other games involved getting all balloons of one color to the other side of the room before the other team. Some kids were on offense and the rest were on defense. Rebecca thought these kids would sleep well tonight, allowing their parents to enjoy the ball drop at midnight alone.

A pre-approved pizza lunch buffet was donated by the Newfound House of Pizza, and then it was time to start counting. Rebecca had borrowed a huge analog wall clock from a local store for the countdown to noon. Each child picked up their poppers, hats and necklaces before shouting out the last moments of the party.

"Three, two, one... Happy New Year!" Twenty little heads bounced up and down to the song Happy by Pharrell.

"Anyone else ready to head home?" Mary asked of the other two adults when a couple songs had played through.

Both Jeremy and Rebecca raised their hands.

"I'll clean up the room if the two of you want to bring the kids out to the parents," Jeremy offered.

"That's a deal," responded Mary for the pair of them. She grabbed Rebecca's hand and started walking in the direction of the doors back to the rest of the library.

"Let's go, kids," Rebecca called. "Your parents will be here any minute."

The process to sign out with parents took around fifteen minutes. When they checked on Jeremy, he had just finished putting away the tables and chairs.

"I hope you both have a wonderful evening." Rebecca had already learned Mary was staying home to read and Jeremy was going out with a few friends for dinner.

"I hope your first New Year's Eve with Kenny is magical," Mary said, batting her eyelashes.

"We'll be meeting at The Glacial Inn. Kenny secured us a table reservation."

"Why isn't he picking you up? Kenny seems to be quite the gentleman," Mary commented.

"Ladies, I'll see you in the new year," Jeremy interrupted. "Enjoy your gossip."

Mary huffed. "We are not gossiping. I'm asking Rebecca about her date tonight."

"My apologies. Enjoy your chat." He walked through the doors and out to his car, throwing a wave over his shoulder along the way.

"Back to the question," restarted Mary. "Why isn't he picking you up?"

"Two officers recently took other jobs, so Kenny has to be available tonight in case something happens. With it being New Year's Eve, he's worried especially about accidents due to unsafe driving and the potential weather conditions."

The weather was good at noon, but there was a high probability of snow while they were on their date. Rebecca trusted herself as a safe driver, but not everyone made good choices when it came to driving on New Year's Eve.

"I'm sure it will be perfect anyway. Are you ready to leave?"

"I just need to return the clock, then I'll head home to get ready. Get going on your restful evening."

Mary pulled her winter jacket on over her glittery outfit. "That I will, dear. See you next year." The two women hugged and smiled as they looked each other in the eye for a moment before splitting up. Rebecca walked back to the multi-purpose room as Mary let herself out, carrying a copy of Midwinter Murders, by Agatha Christie.

The returning of the clock took only moments on her way home. When she got there, her cats were nowhere to be found. "Joey? Bean? I'm home." There was no sound to imply her cats were coming to find her, which she thought was odd. Typically, she was holding her cats back from escaping when she opened the front door, but not today.

Before heading upstairs to shower and get ready for the party, she knew she had to find them. Walking into the kitchen, she saw the door to the basement ajar. "Of course." The cats were not permitted to go into the basement because her house was so old and she was worried they could get stuck or injured. It didn't appear to Rebecca that there was any way to get out of the house through the basement, but if mice could get in, she must have been wrong.

She took the stairs down to get their attention with a bag of treats. She shook and rustled the bag and called out their names. "Joey! Bean! Let's get treats!" She continued making noise on the way up, eventually being followed by the two black cats. They were covered from head to tail in cobwebs, but otherwise seemed fine. "You two. What am I going to do with you?" she asked as she closed the basement door.

Their purrs didn't answer the question, but she knew she had promised them treats to get them back upstairs. She dropped several in front of each cat, knowing Joey would probably finish first and try to steal one or two from Bean.

She had a long time to wait before the dinner started, so she walked upstairs and checked on the outfit she had already checked on three times that morning. The form-fitting silver dress that had a slit up the leg hung on the open closet door. This dress was her final choice because she liked the way it looked with her auburn hair. She hoped Kenny liked it as much as she did.

A shower and a blow dry were the primary order before makeup and getting dressed, but she was still hours from pulling back out of her driveway. Considering she had missed watching it on Christmas Eve, she figured it was almost as fitting to watch The Holiday on New Year's Eve. She put on sweatpants and an oversized t-shirt to curl up on her couch to watch the movie with her cats, maybe even sneaking in a small nap, just trying to pass the time before her highly anticipated date with the police chief.

Chapter 2

The During

Rebecca finished her movie and puttered around, checking the clocks over and over again. Since the reservations included assigned seating, and she could arrive as early as half past eight, she left her house at quarter past. Before pulling out of the driveway, she sent a text to Kenny.

Rebecca: Leaving now.

Rebecca: Can't wait to see you!

The drive past the foot of the lake proved just how warm the winter had been so far. The lake was far from freezing over, and ice fishermen would be getting antsy starting tomorrow when they would have otherwise been able to start. It wasn't much further, past Catch of the Day and The Ledge, until she caught sight of Once Inn a Lifetime. There were so many tragic yet fascinating memories on this one stretch of road for Rebecca. This year sure had been full of unexpected events.

When she was almost to the Mom-and-Pop Shop,

home of the Turkey Trot, she turned into a parking lot on the opposite side of the road. The Glacial Inn was originally built in the early 1800's and had been modified and added to over the years. The parking lot was full of the cars of dinner guests, not ones staying until midnight, who were leaving now that the party was about to start.

As a car pulled out of a spot near the front door, Rebecca waited patiently to pull in. Her satin heels were a poor choice for getting to and from her car given the slush in the gravel parking lot. Though it would ruin the look if Kenny happened to be waiting for her just inside the door, her practical side took over. She pulled on her winter jacket and Muck boots and exited the car, carrying her heels and clutch in her left hand, keeping her right hand free in case she fell.

Once inside, she quickly hung up her jacket, removed the boots and slipped on the heels. Though they were not typically in her wardrobe, she was capable of maneuvering in heels, a skill retained from high school. The space she currently occupied was covered from wall to wall in Polaroid photos from special events spanning many, many years. The staircase on her right led up to The Gin & Tonic Tavern, also known simply as The GINN. There were reserved seats up in the bar, and a DJ would be performing up there soon.

Rebecca knew, however, that the seats Kenny had reserved for them were on the first floor and in the room that would be hosting a live band. The theme for the New Year's Eve party was Elegant Eighties. The advertisements suggested making and thrifting eighties themed elegant party looks. Rebecca didn't know how to do anything halfway, so not only was she rocking a fully sequined dress that weighed more than any outfit she had ever owned, but her crimped side ponytail was totally awesome. The icing on the cake was a pair of black satin gloves that went up beyond Rebecca's elbows ending in matching bows. The only thing that could ruin this epic outfit was if Kenny didn't also play along.

When the door opened, allowing a blast of cold air to hit her bare shoulders, in walked the man of her dreams. Chief Kenny Towne had changed out of his uniform and into a white tuxedo with a white bowtie, white vest and shiny white shoes to match. In his hand, he held a plastic container with a wrist corsage sporting pink carnations and Baby's Breath.

"You wouldn't tell me what your dress looked like, so I had to guess on my outfit. Sorry, but the pictures are going to be awful." He held out the plastic box. "I got you this."

"This couldn't be more perfect." She was in awe of the commitment to the theme but also the overall effort. Kenny had applied a fake mustache to complete his outfit. "I thought sourcing a crimper would win me bonus points, but the mustache wins." They laughed together, embracing in a hug before the door opened again, requiring them to move further into the restaurant.

The woman behind the counter held a clipboard containing a list of the people with reservations. "Chief Towne. I feel safer with you here tonight."

"Well, I brought Rebecca with me, so that may even

things out. She can be quite the bad penny, if you haven't heard."

Rebecca smacked him in the arm with her clutch. "I resemble that accusation."

"We've got good seats for the two of you near the band," she interrupted. "Hope you wore your dancing shoes." As she turned the corner of the counter, ready to escort them to their seats, she looked down at their footwear. "Chief Towne, I do hope you get to stay for the whole event. If you show up on any scene in that outfit, the criminals might laugh themselves to death."

"I'm just here to support a Newfound area business on a holiday. You said Elegant Eighties, and I ran with it." Kenny shrugged and tossed up his hands.

Rebecca swiveled her head side to side as she walked through the first room, which wasn't typically filled with tables, but was tonight for the big celebration. The Glacial Inn needed to make use of every square foot to accommodate those who wanted to party. To her right, she could see the buffet, and she scoped out what she wanted to start with. When she crossed through a doorway into the long dining room, Rebecca observed that it was lined with floor to ceiling glass and had tables that sat large groups, but no small tables for a party of two. The center of the room was filled with tables for eight, while the side tables had room for six each.

"Will we get our own table?" Rebecca asked.

"Not for the party. We use these longer tables to maximize seating, and you'll be with other couples or groups."

This wasn't a situation Rebecca was prepared for. She envisioned a romantic date night after a long month of waiting. Now, she was preparing to be seated with a group of strangers.

"Here you two go." The woman placed name cards on the two seats at the end of a table for eight. "These seats are yours for the night. You can come and go between the buffet as many times as you like, and The GINN is open as well. All seats are assigned, but you can sit if it's open. Just be respectful if someone comes back to their seat. Okay?"

"Sounds good. Thanks," responded Kenny. They took their seats.

"Plates are up at the buffet when you're ready, and waitstaff will be around to take your drink orders. Enjoy." She walked back in the direction of the front counter to seat the couple who entered behind Kenny.

Over the next twenty minutes, Kenny and Rebecca helped themselves to steak and seafood as well as a variety of sides. They went back up for a second helping, and Kenny had already reached the buffet when Rebecca ran into Reese.

"Reese, I can't believe you got out of your own kitchen." Her restaurant, Jilly's, wasn't open in the evenings, and she was accompanied by three of her waitresses.

"Girls' night out. Husbands and boyfriends not invited," Reese hollered as the women behind her cheered. "We're here to celebrate Andrea Devine's divorce. Tonight, she's the toast of Newfound!" She pointed to the woman wearing a sash that read 'Newly Single.'

"Sounds like a plan. I'll see you on the dance floor. By the way, nice sequins," she complimented Reese.

Reese wore a gold dress with an oversized bow on one shoulder, gold sequins on the torso and layers upon layers of shiny gold fabric that created an above-the-knee skirt. "Thank you. I'm living my best eighties life."

"Ladies. This way," called the annoyed hostess.

"Whoops. Guess we're supposed to be following her. See you later." Reese and the three women decked out in neon tracksuits and spandex took off.

When Rebecca stepped up to meet Kenny at the buffet, she said, "Just ran into Reese. Wonder who else we'll know tonight."

"I'm sure I'll know most of the people. I just hope there's no one I've arrested lately." He winked.

Rebecca scooped shrimp onto her plate along with another helping of bacon-wrapped scallops. Kenny's plate was full of pigs in a blanket and chicken wings.

They returned to their assigned seats only to find four of the seats at their table were now occupied by the women from Jilly's. The four of them cheered when Kenny and Rebecca joined them.

"Now we're representing all kinds of eighties fashion together," said Andrea. She also had a side ponytail, but her bangs were the real eighties feature. Teased within an inch of their life, the bangs stood at least five inches above her hairline.

"I feel better that I know you," stated Rebecca, letting

out a sigh of relief. "Can you hand me two of those bags, please?"

The center of the table had eight gift bags filled with hats, tiaras, necklaces, glasses and other party favors. The part that made Rebecca smile were the Christmas crackers in the bottom, obviously intended for midnight.

By this time, the band had started playing an assortment of eighties hits. Dinner plates had long been removed, and Rebecca had already Pumped up the Jam, had a Total Eclipse of the Heart and Beat It along with the girls from Jilly's before she and Kenny made their way up to The GINN to check out the DJ.

The stairs that led up to the second-floor bar were lined with old license plates and a corkboard filled with local information. Almost everything in the bar was made of wood aside from the carpet and television screens. The DJ was playing current hits as they stood at the bar to get sodas in champagne glasses. With the possibility of getting called in, Kenny wasn't about to risk drinking tonight, nor was Rebecca. Since she took her own car, she'd need to drive home after the ball dropped.

They didn't stay long because the music was difficult to talk over, and they both preferred the nostalgia of listening to hits from when they were in school. The dance floor downstairs was still hopping when they sat down with their drinks and found Jon and Patty Williams at the far end of their table.

"What are you two doing, getting here so late? You've missed so much dancing." She had to shout over the volume of the band.

"Problems at the new coffee shop. We'll get it sorted soon, I hope," said Jon. "It's always something."

Rebecca lifted her glass and moved down a couple seats. Reese and her entourage were still dancing, so the chairs between them were empty. Kenny stood and wandered around to other tables after waving in the direction of the couple.

"It's nice to see you again. I'm sure business has been good," Rebecca encouraged.

Jon and Patty had just opened their coffee shop, Journey, in the middle of town. Rebecca remembered how beautiful the exposed wooden beams and open space were from her one trip in to get a hot chocolate. She didn't drink coffee but wanted to show her support for the new business.

Jon pointed at her and said, "We got the mini marshmallows in, just like you asked for."

"Good to know. I'll make sure to stop in again soon."

Time flew by and Rebecca was searching for Kenny when the band announced there was only one minute until midnight. She had added the tiara to her hairdo a while ago, and she had a hat in her hands for Kenny. She couldn't believe they might miss their first New Year's Eve kiss. With twenty seconds to spare, he swooped in to pop the hat on his head and toast to the new year.

"May we be just starting our adventures together. Here's to a simpler year with fewer curveballs." They both raised their glasses of ginger ale.

"Three, Two, One... Happy New Year!"

Everyone was grabbing for the Christmas crackers

and creating a cacophony of bangs and cracking sounds around them as Kenny leaned in for a confetti-covered kiss. He dipped Rebecca in a slow bend, supporting her at the shoulders with a free hand and waist with his forearm while she placed a hand over her tiara to keep it from falling off. A series of screams woke them from their bubble.

Kenny stood, which quickly righted Rebecca, causing her to wobble a little on her heels when she quickly felt lightheaded. They both looked around and spotted three of the women from Jilly's pointing at the ground between their table and the dance floor.

Considering the dim lighting and the dark floor, a pool of slowly moving liquid spreading across the wood wasn't immediately apparent. Andrea's body was lying face up with a shocked look frozen on her face. The front of her purple and pink tracksuit looked like the paint splatter pants that had been popular in the eighties, with the exception of a crimson bloom across her chest.

"Everybody down," shouted Kenny above the celebration.

Chapter 3

The After

REBECCA DROPPED ONTO THE FLOOR NEAR HER chair. While she had helped Kenny on no fewer than seven investigations this year, she wasn't about to ignore his command. Suddenly, her field of view had been limited to the people immediately next to her and those on either side of the tables. She could see Andrea's body through the legs of the table and chairs they had just been celebrating around. Reese appeared to be checking on her while Kenny surveyed the scene.

A member of the band had jumped in to attempt to stop the bleeding with a piece of green and red fabric that had been draped as a decoration. Rebecca watched Kenny's eyes stop on the situation long enough to register the action.

"Stay down while I go check things out," he instructed in Rebecca's direction, never taking his eyes off the rest of the room as he scanned. He took his cell phone out of his back pocket and proceeded to leave the dining room.

To her right were two of the waitReeses from Jilly's and the Williams couple from the coffee shop. She crawled past the two women holding each other and approached Jon. "Did you see anything?" she whispered.

"Nothing. You?" he hissed, Patty beside him.

"No. I was facing the band then kissing Kenny. She was in my peripheral vision before midnight, but not my focus."

Rebecca tried to look through the table and chair legs again in Andrea's direction. Reese was laying across her body and silently shaking while the band member continued to apply pressure to the area that had turned crimson.

"I was kissing Patty, so I wasn't looking at her either."

"Same," added Patty. "I mean, I was kissing Jon."

"Someone saw something. We just need to find out who."

Jon warned, "Chief Towne said to wait here. I'm sure he'll accept your help when the time is appropriate." Jon had been there just a few short weeks earlier when she helped solve a murder at Santa's Village.

Waiting wasn't her strong suit, but Jon was right. Kenny returned after what was probably a couple minutes, but it felt like an hour had passed. His eyes again looked to the scene between the band and his table. The man holding the fabric to Andrea's chest shook his head side to side but remained in place.

"We would like everyone to take their assigned seats.

If your assigned seat is not in this room, please stay standing." Everyone followed his orders except Reese and the guitarist. Sirens could be heard approaching. With his back to the entrance of the dining room he said, "Everyone will be questioned and searched before you are allowed to go home. Leave all cellphones where they are. I have additional officers on the way. Please sit on the floor where you are if you do not have an assigned seat in this room."

"Can we stand?" asked a partygoer Rebecca didn't recognize.

"Yes, just stay where you are," responded Kenny. He purposefully walked over to Rebecca and leaned down to where she was now sitting in a chair instead of kneeling on the floor. "I won't have an officer here for a couple minutes," he whispered in her ear. "Write down if you notice anything suspicious or anyone changing their location." She looked down at his hand on the table. When he stood, a pen and small pad of paper remained.

Recognizing the importance of the request, she didn't move to grab it. Most of the people in the room were watching their interaction, so she didn't want to alert anyone who might give something away.

Chief Towne stood and returned to the entrance of the dining room. At the same time, EMTs entered the restaurant. Their commotion couldn't be mistaken for anything else due to the sirens and gear. When they dropped to Andrea's side, they confirmed what the guitarist had hinted at.

"She's gone," the tallest of the EMTs reported.

The wailing from Reese and the two other waitresses became overwhelming. Reese, now unable to hug or console the remaining coworkers due to the state of her clothing, didn't bother to rise from the floor. Rebecca turned to look at the rest of the room. Everyone was staring back in the direction of the women who were inconsolable.

Rebecca made mental notes of those not paying attention and those who looked particularly antsy. When she turned back around, she tried to subtly write down those observations. When she looked back up, a familiar face was staring at her.

Assuming she was wrapped up in her date, she hadn't noticed the newspaper reporter seated two tables behind her to her left. Giovanni Bianchi was fuming in his seat, practically twitching as he glared at her.

"We'll take Reese, you, sir, and the two women that came with you, Reese. Please, follow me." The EMT helped Reese up, and she walked with the guitarist out of the room, followed by the two other women.

"We are going to be here for a while," she said down the table to Jon and Patty. "Even if they bring in extra officers, they have over one hundred people in here to talk to."

"You think?" Patty asked. "Why so many?"

"There will be waiters and waitresses, the owners, the people on this floor and whoever is upstairs in The GINN."

"But why would they interview people upstairs?"

Rebecca inhaled deeply and let out the breath.

"Before we noticed Andrea had fallen, someone could have left via the front door or gone upstairs to get an alibi." She changed her voice to sound more masculine. "No, sir, I was up here when they counted down to midnight." Back in her normal voice she finished her thought. "If the person who killed Andrea wasn't with anyone, people probably wouldn't have paid much attention. Look at us." She waved a hand back and forth between them. "We were closer than anyone, and we weren't looking at her or anyone other than our partner. Midnight was a great distraction." They both nodded.

When Kenny reentered the room, still in his white tuxedo, he curled his index finger to call Rebecca over to him this time. She caught Jon and Patty's eyes before standing and walking out of the dining room with him.

"See anything yet?" he asked.

"I really can't be sure, but no one was moving around to change their position. Why? What happened to her?"

"She was shot."

"That's ridiculous. We would have heard it." This time, she swatted her clutch into his chest."

"Would we? With all of the noise the band started to make and those cracker things going off everywhere? I know a gunshot when I hear one, and I never heard one."

"I suppose that's true. It did get very loud as soon as it hit midnight," recalled Rebecca.

"How long can you stick it out with me tonight?"

"As long as you need. I rested between the library party and tonight. What can I do?"

"The best thing you can do is be my eyes and ears in

the dining room. I can't be in there while I'm asking everyone questions. Try to chat, where you can, but observe."

"I can do that. Want me to go back in?"

"Please."

When she returned, she noticed a police officer moving from person to person, writing something down. "Jon, what's she doing?"

"Best I can guess, she's writing down names of everyone here."

"Why bother? That seems like a waste of resources." Rebecca watched the officer pass quickly from person to person from the seat next to Patty.

Patty spoke up. "Well, some people aren't in their reserved seats, some didn't make reservations, and some are probably going to show up as missing. This way, the other officers know if there are any red flags."

"That's impressive, Patty. I bet you're right," Rebecca agreed.

On the far side of their table, an officer was already taking photographs of the scene, and the EMTs were waiting off to the side to remove Andrea's body. It was unsettling to think about just how little it bothered Rebecca to sit so close to a corpse. Patty was now sitting on the same side of the table as Jon, but they had both turned their chairs so they weren't looking in Andrea's direction.

"What do we know about Andrea?" Rebecca asked in their general direction.

"We've seen her in Jilly's before. While we were

trying to get the coffee shop up and running, we had many meals there. It wasn't far down the road, and it meant we didn't have to drive all the way home," Jon summed up.

"Yeah, we don't know her outside of the restaurant."

"Did you notice she was here celebrating her divorce?"

"I saw the sash," recalled Patty, "but that's all. Did you know her?"

The use of the word 'did' stung. Rebecca often got caught up in the moment, and Patty said something that brought her right back down to Earth. Andrea was gone. They were talking about her in the past tense. Straightening up, she replied, "Only from Jilly's. I saw them come in tonight, and they were celebrating the divorce being finalized with a girls' night."

"I bet he'd be a suspect," said Jon.

"There is no way he'd be here tonight, right? Kenny, I mean Chief Towne, has to know to look for him, but he may not even know who her ex-husband is. I don't."

"They took Reese out first to interview her, so I'm sure she'll give them information about him. Oh, I hope he wasn't here tonight. Everyone will assume he's guilty," Patty worried.

"That's why they investigate," Jon soothed.

"Rebecca, fancy meeting you here," came a female voice from behind. Rebecca spun in her seat to see the officer walking around the room had arrived at their table.

"Do I know you?" she asked.

"Possibly not, but I certainly know you. Chief Towne talks about you often."

Rebecca felt heat rise up her throat to her cheeks. She looked down at the interesting outfit she had chosen for the night. "I promise I don't always dress like this."

"I'll reserve judgement for now," joked the officer with a badge reading Boggs. "Now, is this your assigned seat?"

Rebecca pointed to the end of the table. "Kenny and I had the two outer seats, one on each side of the table."

"And, what were you doing at midnight, as if I need to ask?" Boggs nudged Rebecca's shoulder with her elbow, in a gesture usually reserved for friends.

"I was kissing. I didn't see anything until Andrea was already on the ground."

"Were you kissing here, at your seats?"

Rebecca rolled her eyes. "We were both on this side of the table so we could watch the band. We were standing."

"Thank you. Please do not leave the building until you've spoken to one of the interviewing officers, but you are free to move about the room or use the bathroom."

"Thank you."

The officer moved on to ask the same questions of Patty and Jon then other partygoers.

"Now, we wait again," announced Jon.

"At least it appears you were right, Patty. Taking names and asking where we were in the room. Now, do you have any idea what actually happened to Andrea?"

Patty and Jon both looked puzzled. Jon responded

first. "She just fell. I wasn't looking at her, but when we stopped kissing, I saw her falling and land. Reese got to her so quickly, and the band guy too, I didn't move. Not that I had much to contribute."

"I only saw her after she was already on the ground. So sad." It appeared to Rebecca that Patty also had a moment of realization that a person had died.

"What a way to spend New Year's Eve. Here I was, planning on a romantic date night, and I ended up part of another investigation."

"Well, well, well."

A voice Rebecca knew immediately made the hair on the back of her neck stand up. She stood and turned to face Giovanni Bianchi about two feet from her face. "What do we have here? The librarian assisting her boyfriend at the scene of yet another murder. I'm going to start wondering how you're always in the right place at the wrong time."

Chapter 4

The Scramble

"Mr. Bianchi, I can assure you I would much rather be dancing and enjoying my evening than this." Rebecca gestured to the floor in front of the band where Andrea had landed. "Who would ever want to be in the right place at the wrong time, as you so eloquently put it. I'd argue that I'm at the wrong place considering my date isn't even here."

"I'm sure the deceased is feeling very badly about ruining your date." He smirked and one eyebrow rose. Rebecca wasn't a violent person, but if anyone could cause her to slap someone in the face, it was him.

"You took that completely out of context. I'm surprised you don't have a camera with you, ready to break the story tomorrow morning."

"I do have my camera, but we were told to leave our phones where they were. Staying on Chief Towne's good side is a priority if I want to get an exclusive for the paper."

Rebecca wanted to throw up all over his stonewashed jeans and Miami Dolphins jacket with the snaps. His white high-tops with the tongue sticking out were enough to make her think of the phrase 'Gag me with a spoon.' She wondered where he was able to get such throwbacks because they looked authentic.

"Why don't you ask what you want so you can get on with your night. I'm not interested in being harassed by you."

"Fine. Did you see what happened to the victim? You were very close."

"If you were watching from your seat, you'd have seen me kissing when the countdown ended. From where we were, neither Chief Towne nor I could have seen her death."

He held up a pen to his lips and tapped it at the corner. "You say death. Do you know how she died?"

"How would I know? She had blood all over the front of her tracksuit, so that can't be good."

"Well, did you see or hear anything before you noticed her?"

"Giovanni, why are you asking me so many questions?" She placed her hands on her hips. "Clearly I didn't do anything, so why not go ask others some questions.

"Look, I'd be a fool to not want to know what you know. You've been closer to the big stories all year than I have, and I realized I was approaching this the wrong way. Maybe we can work together."

Rebecca stared at him, deadpan. "Maybe not." She

turned around and sat in her assigned seat, determined not to look at him. After several minutes passed, she tried to look over her opposite shoulder to maybe catch a glimpse of him in her peripheral vision. It appeared he was gone. She sighed, happy he was no longer bugging her, but disappointed she had wasted so much time on him.

Rebecca thought to herself that there must be plenty of people here she knew, and maybe she should be making the rounds, looking for anyone suspicious and asking a few questions of her own. When she looked behind her once again, she spotted Adam Odrezak, owner of The Ledge. Since summer was clearly over, he was technically unemployed. His restaurant wouldn't be open again for several months. On his arm, and wearing an annoyed look on her face, was a woman many years younger than Adam. Rebecca took it upon herself to walk two tables back to talk to them.

She approached with her arm outstretched. "Adam, nice to see you again," she cooed, trying to get on his good side. "I'm glad we were able to wrap up everything at your place this summer."

"What is she talking about, Ace?" The petite woman wrapped her slim arms around his right bicep. "Who is this?"

He cleared his throat, shaking her off so he could accept Rebecca's hand. "This is Rebecca Ramsey. She's the librarian in Bristol, and she dates the police chief. She has helped me at the restaurant before with a delicate situation. I don't need to ask how your night is going."

"Yours either. You're stuck here just like the rest of us."

"I'm confident Kenny will move us along shortly. I caught his eye when he was in here last."

"I'd be confident he'll do his job thoroughly. If you notice, the people at the back have all spoken to the police first. You're in the middle of the room. I'd sit tight."

Adam looked behind him quickly, and his face sank as he turned back to Rebecca."

"I see. Well, what do you know?"

Rebecca wanted to know why everyone assumed she knew things. "Not much. Didn't see anything important, not at least that I know of. You?"

"I will say that I heard what I thought was a gunshot earlier, but with all that noise going off, I figured I was just making it up in my head. Do you know if she was shot?"

"Let's assume I don't know if she was shot," Rebecca said. "But if I wanted to pretend that she was, where might that sound have come from?"

"My right and back. It sounded like one of those Christmas crackers from the bags, but different somehow. I guess I've heard enough gunshots to be aware."

"That's really helpful. Make sure to let Chief Towne know that when you speak to him, or whoever interviews you. Really a tragedy for tonight to end like this."

"Excuse me. I need to use the powder room." Adam's date got up, checked in with the officer near the entrance to the dining room, and exited.

Adam corrected her. "It's a horrible way to start the

new year. I was here on a first date. Guessing it will be my last."

"I wouldn't be so sure. She doesn't seem all that broken up. Does she know you own The Ledge?"

"I suppose she does. Why?"

Rebecca shook as a single snort escaped her mouth. "I'm sure she'll give you a second chance if she knows that. You're a good guy who owns a, shall we say, lucrative business that's only open half of the year. Women probably overlook certain things for your other qualities."

"I'm not sure if I should be offended, Rebecca."

"Absolutely not. You *are* a good guy, but the restaurant doesn't hurt your chances." Rebecca inched closer and lowered her voice. "She's a lot younger than you."

"HA! Not that much. We're just having fun."

Rebecca rolled her eyes. "Just be careful with your heart and your wallet."

The young woman returned. "I hope you weren't talking about me, Ace." She snuggled back up to his arm and nuzzled her nose to his cheek.

"Rebecca and I go way back. We were just catching up. Did I mention she dates the police chief, Chief Towne?" Rebecca could tell he was trying to change the subject.

"Oh, I bet he makes a good salary. Is he busy a lot?"

Rebecca gave Adam a knowing look then pinched her lips together to prevent her grin from showing through. "He is quite busy, and he has two little girls and an ex-wife. I have my hands full."

"That sounds like a lot to balance. Adam here is a

free man with the world at his fingertips, aren't you, Ace?"

Adam dropped his head and shook it from side to side. "I guess I am. Rebecca, I hope you are able to go home soon and follow up with Kenny about that sound. Someone might want to search the building and the guests."

Rebecca's jaw dropped. She stood, retrieved her clutch from her table and moved toward the exit. Realizing this had been a rude way to leave the conversation she stopped and turned back around. "Nice to see you. If you get to leave first, have a nice night and a happy new year." She walked quickly but purposefully in the direction of the front counter. Kenny was meeting individually with witnesses, before they were allowed to leave, in the office typically occupied by the owner.

An officer Rebecca was very familiar with was standing guard between the office entrance and the door to exit the building.

"Jacob, I need to talk to Kenny, uh, Chief Towne."

"Sorry, Rebecca, but he's in the middle of an interview. I can't let you in there."

"Jacob, come on. You know as well as I do that if I'm here, it's worth the interruption."

He paused to think. "No, he said not to be interrupted."

Rebecca opened her clutch and took out her cell phone. She tapped the screen a few times and placed the phone to her ear.

"Hey, I need to talk to you, and your guard dog won't let me in." Seconds later, the door to the office opened.

"What can I help you with, Rebecca? Jacob, can you finish up with Donny?"

"Yes, sir."

"Donny? I never saw him here tonight," she commented.

"What did you need Rebecca?" Kenny looked and sounded irritated, probably realizing he shouldn't have mentioned who he was currently speaking with.

"I was just talking to Adam about a sound he heard. He's sitting about halfway between the band and the back of the room. He thought he heard a gunshot over his right shoulder. You may want to talk to him soon. He also suggested people should be searched before leaving, and the room should be searched, but I haven't seen anyone checking the room. Are you going to do that?"

He looked down at her, never losing eye contact. "Rebecca, we know it was a gunshot wound. Of course, we are searching people. We will search the room when it is empty, and we have an officer watching the room as well."

"Yes, but you've started to let people move about. If the killer had a reserved seat upstairs, they wouldn't have been searched before going up and could dispose of evidence somewhere else in the building."

Kenny looked at Rebecca, then to the door of the establishment.

"How many people have you already let leave?"

"Dozens."

"And are they all from the back of the room?"

He hung his head. Facing the floor he replied, "Yes."

"How can I help?" she offered.

"Nothing, really. Finding the weapon will be important, but we've also been testing everyone's hands for gunpowder residue. The town's going to love that bill. Once someone is questioned, we escort them out and test them outside so no one still inside knows what is going to happen. At least that's one thing in our favor."

"Unless someone in there knows who did it and calls or texts them to warn about the tests."

"It's not perfect, but it's better than nothing. If we get a positive, we clearly will have more questions, but so far, no one has confessed to firing any weapons tonight."

"So, everyone knows she was shot when you ask that. I didn't realize you'd show your cards so quickly."

"We're asking a lot of vague questions that could go in any direction. I feel pretty confident that question will blend in with the rest." He leaned against the counter and sighed. "I'm glad you told me about Adam, and I'll call him in soon. Is there anything else?"

"Oh, you're going to love this." She imitated cracking her knuckles though nothing actually happened. "Giovanni Bianchi is out there and already attempted to intimidate me. So, yeah, that was fun."

"Rompipalle!" He slapped an open hand on the counter.

"What does that mean?" She scrunched up her nose.

"It means I don't like him putting his nose into anything, never mind an investigation we don't really have a handle on. I'll have to figure out something so he doesn't write a first-hand account of the New Year's Eve party gone wrong."

"If he prints this in tomorrow's paper, you'll lose any advantage you may have had."

"I know. Well, the best we can do is get you back in there to watch and listen. I'll call him in before Adam so I can process him and get him out of here."

"I don't mean to make assumptions, but he hasn't broken any good stories in months. Do you think he's a possible suspect? You know, drum up his own story to write about."

"I hope not, but we're not counting anyone out. I know you and I are innocent, and that's all. Everyone else is still a suspect. Thanks for your help. How late can you stay?"

"As late as you need. I can watch the girls in the morning if you or Heather need me to. Just keep it in mind. I'm heading back into the wolf's den. Wish me luck."

Kenny smirked. "You don't need luck. The killer does."

Chapter 5

The Target

REBECCA RETURNED TO THE DINING ROOM, BUT NOT before grabbing a chicken wing off the buffet. She didn't want to dirty an extra plate, so she snagged a napkin instead. Holding it in her right hand, she contemplated what she could do to help while nibbling.

Talking to Giovanni Bianchi was useless, and she was pretty sure she had collected all possible information from Adam. Patty and Jon were huddled over a phone, passing the time. In the front of the room, the band had taken seats and started playing games or doom scrolling on their phones as well. When Rebecca spotted a familiar face up against the glass near the back of the room, she found her purpose.

Passing the officer at the entryway and wrapping the bones up in the napkin, she strode over to a table with Bethany, owner of the bakery Fundamental Elements, sitting against the glass sliders that overlooked the deck. She was wearing an epic power suit in mustard yellow with oversized buttons and enormous shoulder pads. Rebecca waved on the way over, hoping not to surprise Bethany as she took a seat.

"Hey. Long time, no see. How have you been?"

She jumped a little when Rebecca spoke. Clearly, the wave hadn't worked. "Good. I've been good. It's nice to have a little break. I force myself to take some time off this time of year, so I'm here to celebrate New Year's Eve, only it isn't very fun, is it?"

"No, tonight didn't turn out the way I thought it would either," Rebecca agreed.

"Aside from the obvious, how else was today? I saw you were doing a celebration for kids at the library."

"It went great, but I'm regretting it right about now." As the clock was approaching one in the morning, she was starting to recognize the signs of exhaustion.

"I'm sure Chief Towne would let you leave. He's probably your alibi," she joked. "In all seriousness, I would think you'd be the first person he'd let leave."

"I'm sure he would if I needed or wanted to go home, but I'm more interested in helping, if at all possible. Did you see anything?"

"Ugh. I knew you were going to ask me that. The second I saw you leave the room my palms started to sweat."

Rebecca frowned. "I certainly never wanted that reputation."

"Oh, I don't actually mean it in a bad way. I know I didn't do anything, but I also don't think I'll be of any help."

"I guess the only question is about the countdown. How were you celebrating?" Rebecca looked at the empty seats around the table. "Did you come with friends?"

"Sort of. I came with a friend who knew the rest of the table. They all went up to The GINN when we were allowed to move around, but I didn't want to go. I don't really drink and couldn't stand the thought of partying with what happened." Bethany looked to the front of the room and shivered. "The rumor I'm hearing was that she was shot. How could she have been shot and everyone not know it? The first thing I would have done was drop to the floor if I heard a gunshot."

"The countdown had just finished, and everyone was using the Christmas crackers..."

"What's a Christmas cracker?" Bethany interrupted.

Rebecca looked into the bags still strewn on the table and found one with an unused Christmas cracker inside. She held it up for Bethany to see. "This. You pull on the ends and it makes a loud popping sound and confetti and small items come out. I like to compare it to a hand-held piñata. They're popular in England."

"I saw confetti and heard popping, just didn't know where it was coming from, I guess. I had no one to kiss, so I was just shouting and clapping with the others at my table."

"If you didn't hear a gun go off, did you notice anything else suspicious, anything out of place?"

Bethany adjusted herself in the wooden chair that made a loud scuffing sound as she turned. "I did find it odd that someone was moving past the table after the countdown. Usually, people are hugging or kissing, but they stay mostly where they are because they came with people or a significant other. Someone was moving past our table, and I remember thinking it was odd to have somewhere else to be in that moment."

"What did they look like?" Rebecca was feeling like this may be her first real lead.

"I have no idea. I was over here by the window with people in front of and beside me. I feel like they weren't standing up though."

"But you said they were walking or moving. Why would they be standing up?"

"No, it appeared they were hunched over maybe, but I'm not sure. I really didn't get a good look. I wouldn't be of much use in a courtroom, that's for sure."

"Hey, it gives the police something to ask other party-goers about, so you might have an important detail there. You really never know until you have the whole puzzle together." She placed a hand on Bethany's arm that was leaning on the table. "If you think of more, make sure to tell Chief Towne when he calls you in."

"Bethany," called the officer at the entrance. He used two fingers to motion her over to his location.

"There you go. Tell him everything you told me so they can try to fill in the gaps. Maybe the people you came with saw something."

Bethany stood. "I guess I'll get going."

Rebecca got a good look at the suit from head to toe when

she stood. Bethany had even managed to source a three-inch pump in a matching mustard yellow. "Great job on the outfit, by the way. How did you ever find it for tonight?"

"Find it? I had this in my closet. You never know when something will come back into fashion." With that, she passed by Rebecca. "Have a good night." She cringed and apologized after the comment. "You know what I meant."

Rebecca watched her walk away and immediately sent a text to Kenny.

Rebecca: Bethany is on her way in.

Rebecca: She said she didn't hear a gun.

Rebecca: Ask if she saw anyone suspicious.

Three dots popped up, and she waited for the response.

Kenny: Thanks for that last note.

Kenny: Not sure I would have remembered to ask that.

He then sent a winking emoji followed by the one laughing so hard it was crying.

Rebecca realized it was pretty silly to remind the police chief how to do his job, but she was in the heat of the moment. The news Adam had shared about hearing a gun, and the possibility of Bethany seeing someone moving through the aisle had firmly pointed Rebecca's attention in the direction of the back of the room. The only problem with her strategy was the lack of guests still in that part of the restaurant. She glanced to the front to see if her seat was still available and realized she could try to talk to the band, especially the guitarist who tried to help save Andrea.

In the most subtle way a person could saunter in a mirror-ball dress, Rebecca made her way to the front of the room, turning heads along the way. The band, Look What the Cat Dragged In, was an eighties cover band. They primarily performed hair-metal covers, but they threw in some of the big pop and R&B hits as well to keep everyone happy. Every inch of their outfits screamed of boys who grew up listening to Poison, Mötley Crüe, Skid Row, Def Leppard and Warrant. If Rebecca asked them, she guessed they would say it was glam metal. Their target audience were all of the people she had seen and talked to so far.

When she got to the front, she cleared her throat to get their attention. "I just wanted to thank you for your efforts. It's not easy to put yourself in the middle of an emergency like that, and I wanted you to know I appreciated it."

The guitarist who had attempted to save Andrea stared blankly in the direction of Rebecca. "I just did what anyone would do."

"No, you didn't. No one else jumped in like that."

His long hair hung past his shoulders. Black eyeliner that added to the band's image a couple hours ago, bled down his cheeks. "Thank you. I don't feel very good about it." Apparently, he had been allowed to change his clothes when he left earlier with Reese.

"How did you know to grab that fabric? It was a brilliant move in the moment." The need to gain information was a balancing act for Rebecca. If she tried to compliment him, it might make him more likely to talk.

"I saw her fall, which isn't anything new at the places we play." The other band members grunted and nodded in agreement. "At a New Year's Eve party, you almost expect people to be tipsy by midnight. When she didn't hop right back up, I just kept my eye on her. The red on the front of her jacket was the tipping point to jump into action."

"Right, but how did you know what to do?"

"I don't know. Movies. TV shows. I just guessed. It didn't matter, so don't give me too much credit." He watched the toe of his shoe push around a piece of confetti on the wooden floor.

The band had been relocated away from the place where Andrea had fallen, but they could still see the spot and blood on the floor. Rebecca followed the line of sight of other band members who were staring at that location.

This time, the lead singer spoke. "Do you know if the police know what happened?"

"I'm hearing from other people she was shot. Someone even thought they heard a gunshot."

"Wow! That could have easily hit any of us. Maybe one of us was the actual target. Do you think that is possible?"

Not for the first time tonight, Rebecca's mind began to spin out of control. Until about five seconds ago, she was talking about possible motives for killing Andrea. Was it her ex-husband wanting to get even or someone acting on his behalf? Did he hire someone to kill her? Did the motive have everything or nothing to do with her celebration?

Now, Rebecca had four other possible targets with an infinite number of motives. She didn't know these men at all. They were a band out of southern New Hampshire, specifically brought in for the New Year's Eve party. Ads for the party had been up around the lake for months with reservations starting in October. If someone wanted a way to kill a member of the band and be less conspicuous, why not follow them ninety minutes north where they would blend in with a crowd of people dressed in ridiculous outfits?

"Do any of you have a reason to think someone would want you dead?"

The four men looked back and forth between each other.

"I think we've all ticked people off in the past, but I can't think of anything specific. Can any of you?" asked the drummer.

"I'm not sure the police have even considered this possibility. As the members of the band, you were in a set location where everyone could see you and no one was looking backwards. You'd be an easy target, and Andrea could have just moved in front of the intended target as an innocent victim. This adds a whole new dimension."

As Rebecca had just said, the room behind her was significantly emptier than the last time she looked around. Her only guess was that more officers had shown up to go through the interviews quicker. It was getting late, but she was eager to see what the place looked like when it was empty. What had people left behind by accident, and what had people left behind as evidence?

Kenny appeared in the entryway to the dining room. "Excuse me, gentlemen. We'd like to bring you in for an interview, but if it makes more sense to just come to you, we'll have Rebecca leave."

"I'm happy to go somewhere else. No need to ask," she proclaimed. She stood and looked around, recognizing she had her clutch and there was nothing else to collect. "Thanks for talking with me, guys. Best of luck with your band."

She turned and walked in Kenny's direction. Slowing down as she passed, she stated, "Make sure to ask if anyone wanted them dead. What if they were the actual targets?"

Kenny's jaw dropped. "Thanks."

Chapter 6

The Suspect(s)

Rebecca proceeded to walk through the room with the buffet station, now empty and cleaned, and toward the door where she entered and left her boots. She was pleased to find them still near the door, along with her jacket. The stairs that led up to The GINN were partially exposed, and she could hear music coming from the bar. The party was scheduled to stop at one, but legally they could serve until two in the morning. Since the owners needed to stay there anyway, they were probably happy to have some people still contributing financially to their evening.

As she ascended the stairs, she lightly ran her fingers along the antique license plates nailed to the wall and noticed many of them were repeats. She made a mental note to ask another time why that was. At the top step, her toe kicked a recent plate attached to the last riser reading 'THEGINN.'

The music wasn't as loud as it had been earlier, but

there were still a few people dancing in the fenced off dance floor in front of the DJ. She passed the bar and made her way to the back room featuring several empty pool tables and televisions.

"Look what the cat dragged in," said a voice from the far left corner. Watching a television screen replaying a football game from earlier was Donny, owner of The Lakehouse, a gift shop in Bristol. During the summer tourist season, he must have turned a solid profit, but Rebecca figured Christmas was the only other highlight once the tourists left. January through April must have been slow.

"Did you know that was the name of the band downstairs earlier?" she asked.

"Can't say that I did or didn't know." He was sipping a beer, and his table held three empty pint glasses.

"I thought you were seated downstairs because Chief Towne was interviewing you earlier." She didn't know if this mattered, but she might as well slip in a detail letting him know what she had already learned.

"I wasn't interested in that band or the costumes." His speech wasn't slurred, but he was speaking slowly, like it was taking a lot of effort. "The DJ is more my speed." He lifted his pint glass in the direction of the DJ, though he was too far away for the gesture to be appreciated.

Rebecca examined what Donny was wearing – a Red Sox baseball cap, thermal shirt and zip-up hoodie, with a pair of jeans and Timberlands.

"I went downstairs for the countdown because there weren't many options for a kiss up here."

"You thought if you showed up at the last minute, someone would just kiss you?" She scrunched up her face in disbelief.

"Well, my odds weren't going to be worse down there. There were like ten women up here, and they were all with someone. Earlier, I took a quick look in the dining room and there were some all-female groups."

"Did you walk up to the front where the band was right before the countdown?"

"I did, but I didn't find anyone I was interested in, so I kinda bent over for the walk to the back of the room. It was obvious people were trying to see the band around me."

Under her breath she said, "I bet that's who Bethany saw."

"What?"

"Oh, nothing. Just thinking out loud." If it was Donny walking back, the odds of the person Bethany saw being the killer went down drastically. "Did you know Andrea?"

"Andrea who?" He was now inspecting the bottom of his fourth empty pint glass after swallowing the last swig.

"The woman who died tonight. She was a waitress at Jilly's."

"Yeah, I've seen her at Jilly's, but I've also seen her in my shop. She's been in a few times recently."

"Do you see a lot of locals in your shop this time of year for multiple visits?"

48

Donny slowly looked up to Rebecca's face from his empty glass. "No. It's usually a quick stop for a specific gift. I don't see people coming back a lot."

"What has she been buying?"

"Hmmm. What has she been buying?" Donny repeated. Rebecca wasn't confident his memory would be good enough at this time of night and after four beers. "She came in three times and bought the same thing each time."

"What was the same thing?"

"Those keychains with your name on them. I sell a nice leather one with the outline of Newfound Lake on the back and a name on the front. Local guy makes them. She came in three times buying these keychains with different names on them each time."

"Any chance you remember the names or she talked to you about the recipients?" This was a juicy detail. Was Andrea dating and really making the rounds? Her divorce was recently finalized, and there was nothing wrong with her dating, but how many men was she dating currently?

"Nah, but I have a record of it at the store. Need it for inventory purposes. Makes things easier at the end of the year."

"Makes sense. And did you think to tell any of this to the Chief?"

"No. Why would I?"

"Because whoever had received those three keychains could include our suspect. How would you feel if you got the same gift as two other guys in rapid succession. What if she was dating all three of them at the same time?"

"Hadn't given it much thought, but good for her."

Rebecca shook her head. "Well, I wouldn't be surprised if you heard from the police again for the names on the keychains. Oh, I wanted to tell you that I gifted that New Hampshire basket I bought from you in June for a Christmas gift to my Aunt in Ohio. She hasn't been back to the lake in a while, so it was perfect."

Donny was looking toward the bar and not at Rebecca. "Julie!" He waited an extended time before continuing, as if maybe he had forgotten why he called her name. "Can I get another Bud?"

The woman Rebecca assumed was Julie called back to him from behind the bar, "I told you the last one was the last one."

Rebecca snapped her fingers in front of his face. "Donny." He quickly rotated his head to look at Rebecca then held it as if the quick rotation had hurt. "Do you have a ride home?"

"I had a planned ride home, but they have left already."

"I'm going to go talk to Chief Towne. Want me to see if an officer can drop you off at home?"

"Uh, that's probably a good idea. Thanks. I'll stay up here for a while."

Rebecca stood and grabbed her clutch containing her phone. "If they say no, I'll come back up to figure another way to get you home."

"Thanks, Rebecca. You're a good egg."

She left the room and headed back to the stairs that would take her to the first floor. Walking past the bar, she said to Julie, "He's shut off, right?"

"Absolutely. He got that last one about thirty minutes ago, and he's been sipping at it and watching the game ever since." Julie had a bit of a punk rock vibe, but kind eyes behind all of the dark makeup. Rebecca and Kenny had been served by her when they came up earlier, but never caught her name. She was now alone behind the bar, clearly ready to go home for the night.

"Thanks. I'm going to go sort out a ride for him," Rebecca notified the bartender as she started descending the staircase.

"I'll keep an eye out," she shouted back.

When Rebecca reached the first floor, she went in search of Kenny. She found him in the dining room, empty of any partygoers. Rebecca was now the only person not in uniform. While she was upstairs, Kenny must have found a moment to change, though she didn't realize he had brought his uniform.

Standing on the threshold between rooms, she watched the officers take pictures and inspect every square inch of the space. Kenny walked over after a few minutes.

"I can't believe you're still here. I expected you to leave when the dining room cleared out."

"I was upstairs talking to Donny."

"Geesh, I didn't realize he was still here either."

"Yeah, I told him I'd come down to ask if someone could drive him home. He's had too many drinks to drive."

"I really can't spare any officers. We're already down two, and not everyone was available to come in." He looked at his watch. "It's really late, and he'll need to leave here sooner than we'll be ready to go."

"Is there anything I can do to help speed up this part." She knew he'd say she wasn't needed, but something told her to offer.

"I do have one question, but you probably won't know the answer. We're going to need to rely on photos to have any hope of identifying something."

Rebecca watched him walk over near a planter in the corner of the room. "We found this." He held up a satin glove, much like the ones Rebecca was wearing. "Do you remember anyone else wearing gloves like this?"

Rebecca cocked her head to one side, examining the glove. Kenny had removed it from an evidence bag and was holding it in his own gloved hand by the opening that would have gone around the woman's upper arm when it was being worn. The glove hung in a strange way. Down at the fingers, it was oddly shaped as if it still had a hand inside it. Rebecca removed her own glove and held it in the same manner.

"Now do you see the problem?"

The glove she was holding fell limply from top to bottom. The fingers all clumped together as a single pool of fabric instead of still looking like there were fingers inside.

"I don't remember anyone wearing gloves, but something is up with those." She removed her other glove because it felt weird to be wearing one without the other. "Have you checked inside the glove?"

"What would we check inside the glove for?"

"I don't know, but gloves don't do... that." She pointed at the fingers.

Kenny tried to fit his gloved hand inside the opening, but only the first few inches made it inside. His hands were much too large. "Hey, Jacob, can you come try to reach in here?"

"Of course, Chief." He traded for new gloves and joined Kenny and Rebecca standing around the piece of evidence. When he tried to fit his hand inside the opening, it was also too large.

"Rebecca, I know this is unusual, and we'll have Jacob here as a witness, but would you be willing to try?"

"Of course. Anything to help." Jacob handed her a pair of latex gloves. She had watched enough TV to assume it was to not only protect her hand in case there was something dangerous inside, but also to protect any DNA evidence left behind from the person who had worn the gloves to the party.

Once prepared, she placed her smaller hand inside the glove, inching the fabric up like she were going to put in on herself. At the wrist, she felt something squishy. "I can feel something inside. So you want me to pull it out?"

"Yes," said Kenny and Jacob in unison.

As she pulled her hand back out, she removed an

additional latex glove. "Well, doesn't that make things interesting."

"Why would a woman wear a latex glove inside this other glove? I'd think that would be really uncomfortable. Does it make getting them on and off easier?" Jacob looked confused, turning his head side to side like a dog listening to a high-pitch noise.

"This makes me think of something you *won't* find," she responded. "If someone, most likely a woman, was wearing these gloves and had fired a gun, I'm betting they left the party with a negative test for residue like you were testing for. When you get this glove into the hands of someone who can test the fabric, I'm confident you'll find that the outer glove, at the very least, and possibly the inner glove will have the gunpowder residue and not the hand that was inside them.

"Jacob, I need you to drive these immediately to the forensics lab. Call, then call again. Wait outside the lab if you need to so you are the first person in line to get these gloves tested."

"Chief, I doubt they'll be open. It's New Year's Day, technically."

"Fine, drive Donny home. He's upstairs and shouldn't drive. As soon as you drop him off, go to the station and start calling every single contact we have. Call home numbers, cell phone numbers, everything. If you run out of numbers to call, start sending emails. We need to know if these gloves have gunpowder residue on them as quickly as possible."

"And, if I find someone to test them, and they do have gunpowder residue, what's the next step to finding who was wearing them?"

Kenny responded, "Social Media."

Chapter 7

The Names

"Social media?" she asked Kenny, skeptically. "But you told everyone to put their phones down and leave them. I didn't see a single person, not even Giovanni Bianchi, pick up a phone for a picture, and it must have been killing him."

"Yes, but for four hours before that, I guarantee people were taking pictures and posting them all over social media. Heck, I bet the band even posted pictures before midnight."

Rebecca began to ruminate on the possibilities that social media provided. Where would she start? Patty and Jon probably hadn't posted anything, and she didn't see Donny as a slave to social media. "How will you know where to look?" Before she finished the last syllable, she knew what he was going to say.

"We asked, and the list of reservations was provided by the owners." He pointed in the direction of either the counter where people had checked in or the office, but they were right next to each other.

"Makes sense. Well, is there anything else I can do to help here? Donny has a ride, and," she stretched and yawned the next two words, "I'm tired. I should be getting home."

"What are you up to, Rebecca?" His eyes looked her up and down then behind her. "What are you not telling me? I should have kicked you out long ago, but you stuck around to help. Suddenly, you're ready to leave without a fight. What gives?"

"Nothing. My cats are home alone, and I'm sure they are missing me. I thought I could run the kids' party this morning and stay up late, but my old age has caught up with me. Talk after we have both slept?" She looked at him with the most innocent looking puppy dog eyes she could muster.

"I'm still not sure I believe you, but drive carefully. I'll call you in the morning."

"I will. Remember, the library is closed tomorrow, so I have the whole day off. If you find you need me, or you just have a little free time, I'm available. Sorry tonight didn't turn out the way we hoped."

"Me too." He put both hands in his pockets and rocked back on his heels with a loud sigh. "We'll just have to plan another date soon."

"I'll talk to you tomorrow." Rebecca turned quickly and walked toward the door where her boots and jacket waited for her. Along the way, however, she looked over her shoulder. All of the officers were busy inspecting the dining room. She didn't hear anyone on their way down from The GINN either, so she ducked around the counter and grabbed the manilla folder that was sitting on the desktop.

As fast as her fingers could go, she opened the folder to confirm it was the reservation list. She pulled her phone out of her clutch and took pictures of the four-page list. When she closed it and stood, holding the folder below the level of the counter, she searched for anyone looking at her. She appeared to be in the clear, so she replaced the folder to the exact location and angle from where she had procured it and snuck out to the entryway.

While she tugged on her boots and jacket, she looked around at the Polaroids from previous parties. She wished tonight had finished with flashbulbs for a different reason, but she took it upon herself to get a head start on the social media search. Dressy heels and clutch in hand, she attempted to make her way across the gravel parking lot. The weather had held out, so the drive home would be relatively easy. Her car was one of several in the parking lot that wasn't a police car or SUV. Kenny's personal vehicle was still there, and she presumed one or two were the owners' vehicles, maybe even Julie's. Last, she noticed Donny's truck was still in the lot, the same one he parked in front of his shop every day.

When Rebecca walked through her front door, two black cats looked up from their sleeping spots on the couch then lowered their heads back down.

"Are you two really going to stay mad at me?" she

asked. Still in her silver dress, she walked to the kitchen to get wet food for their dishes. Apparently, the sound of the cupboard opening was enough for them to forgive her. "I knew you two would see things my way."

Once they were in front of their respective bowls, she headed upstairs to take a shower and get into pajamas. Her feet hurt from several hours in high heels, so she propped them up on a pillow under the covers and sat back against three pillows to turn on her laptop.

"If I can be forgiven for being so late, you two can be forgiven for your poor attitudes when I got home." Joey and Bean were seated on the floor at the foot of the bed. When she patted the comforter, they both hopped up and started making biscuits. It took the same couple minutes for her laptop to turn on as it did for them to lie down. With her phone by her side, she went onto some of the more popular social media sites, looking for the people listed on the reservation photos she had taken.

"Don't judge me," she reprimanded the innocent felines at the bottom of the bed.

Many of the people listed didn't have social media accounts. The ones who did had mostly pictures of flowers, sunsets and pets. The first one that yielded anything from the New Year's Eve party was one of the waitresses who had sat at her table with Andrea and Reese. Kathy, with a K, was one of the women sporting a tracksuit. She sat facing the band, adjacent to Jon. She had posted some selfies of the group taken before they got to The Glacial Inn, as well as some during the party. The only problem was, there was nothing in the photographs other than the four women. Even the background of the group photos were empty of any useful evidence.

The second name that had a few pictures posted from the party was Patty. While she and Jon had been working late at the coffee shop, they posted a few photos of some new machine they had recently put into operation that the town was going to love, according to them. Rebecca knew nothing about coffee, so it was all over her head. The photo she was interested in, however, showed a familiar face at a table against the window.

A man by the name of Doug sat in the background of Patty's selfie with a long-haired brunette across from him, her back to the band. Rebecca met Doug at a wedding over the summer. He had been the high school best friend of the groom. She had no intention of ever contacting Doug again until, that is, she saw this photo. The woman with her back to the camera was wearing long gloves, similar to Rebecca's. If the tests came back a positive match for gunpowder residue, she'd now be at the top of the list. When she checked the reservation list again, it simply listed Doug's name as a party of two. No one else in the photo was familiar, so a phone call to Doug would be in order tomorrow. She realized, however, that she did have another option.

She opened a window to write a private message to Doug. They had not previously been friends on the app, so she also requested to make them friends. The amount of time it would take for him to see the message was a variable she couldn't control, but she'd be better off sending it sooner than later.

She typed: I don't know if you saw me at the New Year's Eve party, but I don't want you to think I was ignoring you. There was a beautiful woman across from you, and you looked busy. I didn't want to interrupt. I hope your date went well.

With that sent, she continued down the list on her phone. The name Kennedy Wright was quite a distance down the list. Rebecca knew she had a social media presence due to her competitive running, so she started to search. If things were going according to plan, she'd be back to running regularly by now. Kennedy had to withdraw from running the New Hampshire Marathon this year due to a surgery in the spring but was well on her way in September to a full recovery.

She had no problem finding Kennedy's profile online. There were over a dozen pictures posted from the New Year's Eve party, and there was already a post mourning the loss of Andrea, though she wasn't named and there were no details. It seemed from the angle of the pictures, she was seated almost behind the band on the window side of the dining room. As Rebecca scanned the party photos, she found a couple other women wearing gloves but none she recognized and most likely too far forward in the room to be a suspect. Regardless, she saved the photos to her computer so she could send them all to Kenny later.

The funny thing about searching social media for clues was that she didn't really know what to search for. Other than gloves, she didn't have any direction. She knew the murder weapon was a gun, but it's not like the killer would be waving it around in photos. Since most posted photos would likely be from before the murder, she'd be looking for anything that appeared out of place.

Most of the social media posts she found were simply announcing that a couple or group was going out to The Glacial Inn, and some even tagged the location in their post. The last person she looked up was the DJ from The GINN. While the band from downstairs had posted a stock photo of themselves with details of the gig, they had posted no pictures from the actual event. The DJ had not only posted photos every half hour, but he had also gone live during one of his breaks.

Rebecca watched the replay of his live video, which had resulted in very few views, and even fewer comments, and found another familiar face behind the bar. When Rebecca had gone up to talk to Donny, there had only been one bartender remaining. During the video the DJ posted, Joe, the bartender from The Ledge, was also behind the bar. It only made sense that Joe would need to find other work when a seasonal restaurant like The Ledge was closed.

Joe was clearly working as an employee behind the bar on one of the busiest nights of the year, which meant the likelihood of him being the killer was slim to none, but bartenders knew everything. It would be worth a conversation just to find out if he knew any of the gossip from the party. Everyone was allowed to celebrate in any room, so people could have moved around before the countdown. When she looked him up, there was a profile with his name and a picture obviously taken at The

Ledge during the summer. She wasn't friends with Joe either, so she sent a friend request then opened a private message.

She typed: I didn't get a chance to say anything, but I found out you worked the New Year's Eve party at The GINN. Hope all is well!

Much to her surprise, he wrote right back.

Joe: I saw you at the other end of the bar with the chief at one point, but there was no way to get down there. I hope all is well with you too!

Rebecca: Did you hear what happened?

Joe: Second hand. I was still upstairs. Were you in the dining room?

Rebecca: I was at the same table as the woman who died.

Joe: I'm sorry. That must have been awful.

Joe: Does this happen to you as often as it appears?

Rebecca chuckled to herself, briefly annoying the two cats she jostled.

Rebecca: Unfortunately, there does seem to be a pattern.

Suddenly, Rebecca realized there was a whole category of people who weren't on her list.

Rebecca: Hey, you don't happen to know everyone who was working tonight, do you?

Joe: Sure do. Why?

Rebecca: I was checking social media for pictures of the event to see if I was in any of them.

Rebecca: Totally forgot to take any.

Joe: Only employees who may have taken pictures

were the cocktail waitress in the Madonna outfit and the waiter dressed as Michael Jackson.

The rest of the chat was spent catching up on the fall and winter happenings for each of them. It was almost four in the morning when they both signed off. Rebecca felt like she had spent her time productively since leaving the party. Not knowing just how early Kenny would be calling, she decided to set the laptop on the bed to her left, remove two of the pillows from behind her head and scoot down as low as the snoozing felines would allow. Sleep came quickly.

Chapter 8

The Morning

Rebecca woke to a kiss on the forehead.

"You told me to come in, so I did." Kenny was standing over her, holding a bouquet of roses. "I'm sorry my job spoiled last night."

She rubbed her eyes and pulled at her hair, assuming it looked like something between a rat's nest and someone who was recently dragged through a hedge.

"Rebecca, you look beautiful. Come downstairs so we can have breakfast."

"But I didn't buy anything special, and I'm not even sure what I have in the fridge."

"I'm making breakfast," he announced. "Meet me downstairs when you're ready."

Kenny left the room, and Rebecca dashed for the bathroom. Not looking nearly as bad as she imagined, she did need to brush her hair and pull it up in a messy auburn bun. She washed her face and removed the remnants of mascara that didn't quite come off several hours earlier.

Not wanting to go downstairs in her pajamas, she put on a pair of yoga pants, the ones she bought because of a previous investigation, and an oversized sweatshirt reading Emotionally Attached to Fictional Characters. She descended the stairs to find a handsome man in jeans and a plaid button-down shirt. His bare feet made him even more attractive as he moved effortlessly around her kitchen.

"Breakfast is already in the oven and will be out in about fifteen minutes. Want bacon?"

"Is there ever a need to ask that question?" She leaned against the doorframe between the living room and kitchen as he handed her a mug of orange juice.

"I guess not." He placed sheets of paper towel on a dinner plate and started to pull strips of bacon out of the package, laying the strips parallel to each other on top of the paper towels.

"What are you doing?" she asked, admiring the roses he had placed in a vase on the island.

"Cooking bacon. The microwave is a reliable method, and it doesn't stink up the house."

Rebecca smiled. "I've never thought of bacon as stinking up the house."

"If you burn it in a fry pan, it does, and this way I don't have to watch it."

She decided to go along with it considering she wasn't the one cooking. It did hit her as suspicious that breakfast was already in the oven. How long had Kenny been there before he woke her up? Had he been planning to cook her breakfast for a while?

"Can I ask what you are cooking for us?" She looked around the kitchen but found no evidence of packaging or food scraps. Kenny must have cleaned up as he went or just before coming to wake her.

"You can ask, but I'm not telling you until it comes out."

Rebecca was impressed he had already pulled off this much without her knowing. She walked into the kitchen and sat at one of the stools. "Can we talk about last night?"

"This morning, sure."

"Right. I guess it was this morning." Rebecca sipped her orange juice, waiting to see if Kenny would start. When he moved to the refrigerator and pulled out a carton of raspberries and started to wash them, his back to her, she figured it was her turn to go first. "I found several pictures on social media when I got home last night to share with you."

"I knew it. I knew you had a plan when you told me you were tired and wanted to go home." He walked over to her, leaving the raspberries draining in the sink. "What did you do?"

"Someone very irresponsible left the reservation list out on the counter. I may have taken a look at it before heading home."

"That list was on the desktop, not the counter, and I know it was in a folder. Rebecca Ramsey, you're flirting with a thin line here."

"Can I share what I found before you scold me?" If

she wasn't mistaken, he actually growled for a second as he exhaled through his nose.

"What did you find?"

"I'll be right back." She left her mug on the island and hoofed it up to her bedroom where the laptop was still on the far side of the bed. Joey and Bean followed her up the stairs, clearly confused by the events of the morning. She gave them each a little head rub before heading back to the kitchen with her evidence. When she got back, there were two plates on the counter with raspberries on each one and silverware on a folded paper towel.

"I couldn't find napkins," he admitted.

She opened the laptop. "If I even have any, they are probably covered in flags or poinsettias in my basement. I don't really buy napkins, so paper towels are perfect."

"What did you unofficially find last night?"

As she opened a browser, she found Doug had responded to her message from earlier.

Doug wrote: Nice to hear from you. I wish you had said something. I was on a first date, and it wasn't going well. Completely boring, but at least I don't need to worry about a second date. Maybe I'll see you around town.

Kenny leaned on the island, waiting for a response to his question. "The first picture I found had possible evidence in the background of the selfie. Remember Doug from the wedding in August?"

"Yes. What about Doug?"

"His date was wearing gloves like the one you found after the party. I sent him a private message when I got home, after finding them in the picture, and he responded this morning." She showed him the message. "Her name wasn't on the reservation list, so you'll have to dig a little more. Sorry."

"You took a quick look at the list and remembered that?" He tipped his head toward her.

"Let's not ask more questions than you want answers to." She looked back at the screen. "Kennedy Wright also had several pictures including people with gloves in the background. I don't recognize any of them, so you'll need other people to look at them with you. Want me to email them to you?"

"Send all of them to my work address." The beep of the oven alerted him to the breakfast that needed to be removed. Before attending to the oven, he placed the bacon plate in the microwave and started it.

"It smells good. I can't wait to see what it is."

"Keep your expectations low. Mine are. I looked it up online."

"You mean you've never made it before?"

He smiled as he donned mitten potholders and removed a ceramic pie dish from the oven. He placed what appeared to be a ham and cheese quiche on the stove top. "We'll let it cool a little first, and no, I've never made it before."

"Something looks different." She didn't see a traditional crust around the edges, and she really wanted to get up and take a closer look.

"The recipe uses potato shreds to make the crust. What do you think about that?"

She gaped at him then turned back to the breakfast dish on top of the stove. "I think that sounds amazing. I love hash browns, so this sounds great. While we wait, I also talked to the bartender from last night."

"Which one?"

"Joe who works at The Ledge during the summer."

Kenny snickered. "It's a good thing I'm secure in our relationship. You sure do talk to everyone, especially from the past investigations. I didn't get to interview anyone from The GINN. How was Joe?"

"He seemed good. When I was writing in the middle of the night, I was thinking about the band and DJ posting to social media which led me to the people working the event. They aren't on the reservation list, so they also could have posted to social media. Joe gave me some interesting information that goes along with the glove theory."

"What would he have that ties into the glove we found?"

"Not that glove, just gloves in general. What if the person who pulled the trigger was wearing a glove, just not the one you found?"

"What other gloves were worn?" Kenny searched in a drawer.

"What are you looking for?"

"Pie server."

"I don't think I own one. Better go with a spatula."

When he located a spatula and knife, he asked again, "What gloves?"

"Ahhh. Singular. Someone was wearing a singular

glove. Think eighties." She watched as he served up the quiche and practically drooled over the idea of a potato crust. He also removed the bacon plate from the microwave. The bacon actually looked good.

"Maybe just tell me so we can enjoy our breakfast." He went back to serve his piece.

"One of the waiters was dressed as Michael Jackson. Joe said he was wearing the sequined glove. Don't you see?"

Kenny placed bacon on his plate and also on her plate. He then took his plate and sat on his stool, a mug of orange juice already waiting for him. "I understand, but why look for a different glove?"

"Because the glove you have might not have anything to do with the shooting, but any glove could protect hands from gunpowder residue if you were testing people as they left. It's worth looking into, right?"

"Any lead is worth looking into." He stabbed his slice of quiche. "Here we go." Placing the fork of egg, cheese, ham and potato on his tongue, he closed his eyes and his lips. Chewing caused him to moan.

"That good?"

"Try it," he encouraged.

She knew it was going to be amazing, and after tasting the breakfast dish, she also had an involuntary series of sounds escape her throat. "Perfection. The potato on the bottom is the best part. How did you get it crispy but still not at the same time?"

He finished chewing his second bite before answering. "You cook the crust partially before putting in the

71

egg mixture and returning it to the oven. I was doing that part while you slept."

"You can cook me breakfast anytime." She smiled and leaned in for a kiss.

He reciprocated and then pulled back as if she had shocked him. "I just remembered that I spoke to the band, as you suggested."

"Had they come up with any ideas of someone who might want to do any of them harm?"

'Nothing. None of them had crazy ex-wives or debts owed to loan sharks. Unless they were lying to cover something up, I think we can say Andrea was the intended target. Besides, the angle from where Adam thought he heard a shot fired wouldn't make much sense if the person was trying to hit the band. They would have to be one of the worst aims ever to hit Andrea if the band was the target."

"Well, I feel like you have your marching orders of people to look into, and I plan to take the day to relax and read, maybe even take a nap. Glad I never agreed to work for you."

They finished their breakfast in companionable silence. Kenny certainly wasn't going to have a relaxing day, and Rebecca needed him to get going.

"You were a big help, and I appreciate it. Once I take care of these dishes, I'll get going."

"No need. I'll do the dishes because you cooked. That's the way it works, right?"

He smiled. "I guess so. I never get to be on this side. I think I'll stick to doing the dishes though, less work."

Rebecca hopped up and walked him to the door. "Go find that killer." She was putting on her best cheerleader impression in her mind.

"I can't help but feel like you are up to something again."

"Me, never. What would give you that silly idea?" Rebecca swatted her hand in front of her face.

"Evidence. Months and months of evidence. Please, just don't get into trouble I can't get you out of." He opened the front door and put on his shoes that were on the outside step.

"I promise to do my very best to not get into any trouble today."

Kenny held her face in the palm of his hand. "I hope today your best is good enough." He kissed her on the forehead and left.

"Me too," she whispered to herself.

Chapter 9

The Assumption

THE SECOND KENNY PULLED OUT OF THE DRIVEWAY, Rebecca raced back to her laptop. She had completely run out of steam last night when she finished her chat with Joe, and he had given her two more people who may have taken pictures during the party. She searched their names on several apps but couldn't find them. She figured they had private accounts, so she'd need to think outside the box. Where should she go to find out where a waiter and waitress went on a Monday?

Since The GINN would be closed, she tried the next best thing when it came to gossip – Jilly's. Even though she had just eaten a delicious breakfast cooked by her fantastic boyfriend, she figured she could at least put down some home fries and scrambled eggs. After a quick shower and some clean clothes, she was on her way in no time.

The trip to Jilly's was going to be a balancing act. It was Reese who had just lost her friend and employee last night. Rebecca wasn't even sure she would be open due to the tragedy, but it was worth a try. If they weren't open, she'd try another restaurant in town until she found someone with information. When she pulled up in front of the blue and white building, the open sign was in the window. She turned her trusty Subaru off and got out to lock the doors.

The restaurant had a weekday vibe of mostly retired people eating their inexpensive breakfast and drinking their bottomless coffee, but the waitstaff looked worn out. The woman pouring coffee at the counter, Rebecca remembered, was Kathy from the party. She took a seat on a stool and waited to give her condolences.

"Can I pour you a coffee?" Kathy asked, holding a pot of decaf in one hand and high-test in the other.

"OJ, if you have it, please. Large."

"Coming right up." The words were automatic, but the emotion behind them was absent. She walked away to get rid of the pots.

Rebecca hadn't thought about what would happen if Reese wasn't there. It wasn't clear if she was or wasn't at the moment, but she'd need to be prepared to talk to Kathy when she returned.

"What can I get you for breakfast?" she asked, setting down the tall glass of orange juice.

"I'm looking for two scrambled with home fries, please."

"What kind of toast?"

"Cinnamon raisin, please. And, Kathy..." She waited for Kathy to look up from the small pad she was writing on. "I'm really sorry about losing Andrea last night. Kenny and I are both working really hard to find out what happened to her."

"Why are you working on it with the police chief?" There wasn't so much as a hint of a sniffle behind the question; her voice stayed even.

"Well, the police are working on the official investigation, but sometimes I kinda work on things they might not have time for."

"Like what?"

Rebecca was having a hard time reading Kathy. Was she skeptical or truly interested in her answer. "I've been looking for pictures from the party, you know, on social media. I'm sure they can call and stop by the houses of everyone who was at the party last night, but I'm not able to do that. I searched for pictures people posted online once I got home last night."

"Did you find pictures we took?" A new voice came from the front of the restaurant, asking for Kathy. "I'll be right there! Did you find ours?" she asked again.

"I found some, but there was nothing in the background. I was looking to see if there was anything the photos could tell us we didn't already know."

Kathy pulled out her phone. "If that's the case, the ones people post to social media probably won't help." She scrolled through her photos and came to one of the four women similar to one Rebecca saw hours earlier. "People only post the good ones, right? We took several then picked the ones I posted. Look through these." She left in the direction of the voice who called for her moments ago.

Rebecca looked at a photo of the group with the band in the background that hadn't been posted, then there was one closer to midnight when they were dancing. One of the girls was blurry, but the background wasn't. Up against the windows, Rebecca could make out Doug and the brunette, but she was still facing the wrong direction. The table behind him featured a woman dressed as Marilyn Monroe. Rebecca found this odd as the theme was eighties. The blonde bombshell was taking a picture with the waitress dressed as Madonna that Joe had told her about. Rebecca was also able to see the waiter dressed as Michael Jackson carrying a tray of dirty dishes away on the hand with a rhinestoned glove.

When Kathy got back to her at the counter, she pointed to the photo. "Any chance you know the waiter dressed as Michael Jackson?"

"That's Olin. He's a young kid. Works days at Lumberjacks."

"That's great. Thanks."

"Did you still want that breakfast? I haven't put your order in yet."

"How could you tell?"

Kathy smiled, just a half smile, and said, "You looked like you were about to jump off the stool when I told you who he was. If you're going to go find Andrea's killer, the OJ's on me. And whatever you do, don't discount her ex. She just finalized the divorce. I'm sure the news of our celebration had reached his ears. It wouldn't surprise me in the least if he showed up to spoil it."

"Thanks." Rebecca jumped off the stool. "Tell Reese I send my condolences to her as well."

"Will do." Kathy used her pen to salute Rebecca as she left the counter and headed for the front door.

On the drive to Lumberjacks, she wondered what kind of information she could possibly get from Olin, but Joe had said he probably took some photos. If nothing else, she may get a better picture of some people from around the room, gloves or no gloves.

As she walked through the door, a familiar face stood behind the counter on her left.

"Rebecca. What are you doing here? Whatever it is, please tell me I'm not a suspect." Feather, the owner of the Newfound Diner and part-time employee at Lumberjacks, laughed at her own joke. The two met around Halloween when Feather's father had been murdered. Rebecca had helped the police in that investigation as well.

"Unless you were at the New Year's Eve party at The Glacial Inn and I missed it, you're safe. I was wondering if I could talk to Olin."

"Olin!" she shouted. "He's in the back." She motioned to her left. "If you want to go through that doorway, you'll find him organizing something, I'm sure. Good worker. I hope he's not a suspect."

Rebecca didn't answer quickly enough.

Feather gasped. "Olin's a suspect?"

"Everyone that was at the party is a suspect. We have

very little to go on, but I think he may have some evidence that could help."

"Well, as long as he's willing to participate in the investigation, you're more than welcome to go out back and talk."

"Thank you. I appreciate it. Not everyone is so keen to help me help the police."

"That would make me think they are guilty of something. You've done nothing but help around here, and I'd be the first to stand up for you."

"I appreciate that. Back here, you said?" She both moved toward and pointed at the same door Feather had just moments ago, trying to end the conversation at the counter to move on to a more important discussion.

"That's right. Oh, and Happy New Year."

Finally free of the well-meaning Feather, she searched the rows for Olin. Eventually, she found him near a loading dock, unboxing products destined for the shelves of the store.

"Olin, my name is Rebecca. I was..."

"You're the one dating Chief Towne. Saw you at the party last night. Great dress, by the way." He continued to unpack and stack while talking. "Feather told me all about you back when her dad died. After the way last night ended, I wondered if I'd be getting a visit, and here you are."

Rebecca felt good about the ear-to-ear smile plastered on his young face. She estimated Olin to be in his early to mid-twenties based on his positive attitude and lack of wrinkles.

"I saw you last night too. Your Michael Jackson costume was very eighties, glove and all."

"Why, thank you. Feels good to be appreciated. What can I help you with?"

He sure didn't seem like the type to kill a woman and show up to work the next day like everything was fine, but plenty of others had seemed innocent before. "I'm hoping to take a look at any photos you may have taken. Joe, the upstairs bartender, suggested you may have some, possibly on your phone."

"That's right. I was the unofficial photographer last night." His chest puffed up with pride at his proclamation.

"Why is that? Did they hire you to take pictures?"

He laughed. "Nah. I volunteered. It's a good job, don't get me wrong, but waiters always want more butts in the seats. If I take over the social media presence for The Glacial Inn, it can only help my tips in the long run. No one who works there or owns the place does any advertising. They rely on the regulars and people driving by to just pull in. I want to get some life back in the place. Show the locals and tourists what they're missing if they're not stopping by The Glacial Inn for dinner or drinks."

"That's very philanthropic and semi-entrepreneurial of you. I didn't see any photos posted last night, though."

"Couldn't. I was working the event, so I just worried about taking the pictures. I planned to post some when I got home, but it was later than expected and everything went sideways. I was going to talk to the owners about whether they wanted me to wait a bit. See if the police found the killer first. I didn't want it to come off like it didn't matter."

"That's very forward-thinking of you."

They stood in each other's presence for a beat without speaking.

"So, you wanted to see the pictures on my phone?"

"Yes, please. Could we sit down?"

Olin turned over a crate. "You can sit here." He took his phone out of his back pocket and started tapping and swiping. "I'll get you to the pictures, and you can go through them. I'm happy to answer any questions I can, but I have work to get done. Don't want to get behind the first day of the new year."

"I wish all employees took their jobs as seriously as you do. You seem to have a great work ethic."

"I like to think so." He handed the phone over and went back to the case he was previously unloading.

Rebecca started looking through the pictures. In the beginning, most pictures were selfies including Olin. "How did you choose who to take your selfies with?"

His serious face turned to a smile once again. "I asked to take selfies with my favorite outfits. Well, people wearing my favorite outfits."

First was a picture of Olin with his co-worker dressed as Madonna from the movie Desperately Seeking Susan. It wasn't her most famous look, but it was the most appropriate for a waitress working an event. The picture, apparently taken in a bathroom mirror, represented the King and Queen of pop music together again. It held no value to the investigation, so she moved on.

Next, she found a picture Olin had taken with the band, then one with the DJ from The GINN. Both appeared to be taken before the partygoers arrived. Rebecca was confident they had not been the killers, so she swiped to the next photo. For about fifteen pictures, there was almost nothing worthwhile in the background. The one picture she stopped on and found to be the most interesting was the picture of Olin with the woman dressed as Marilyn Monroe.

"Olin, don't you find it odd someone would dress up as Marilyn Monroe for an eighties party?"

"I didn't see anyone dressed as Marilyn Monroe." He stopped working and came over to see what picture she was referring to. "Oh, that's Ms. Hedgecomb. She's not dressed as Marilyn Monroe." He let out a good belly laugh at Rebecca's mistake.

"I also saw her in the background of someone else's pictures taking a selfie with the waitress dressed as Madonna. That's Norma Jean from Gentlemen Prefer Blondes if I ever saw her."

"Ms. Hedgecomb is dressed as Madonna. Don't you remember the Material Girl video where she's wearing a strapless hot pink dress with huge diamond necklaces and bracelets?"

"Do you mind if I send this picture to myself?"

"Go ahead. Does it have something you can use as evidence?"

"I think it might, Olin." She tapped on the screen a

couple times and swiped quickly through the remaining photos. "Thanks. I'm going to get heading out. Really appreciate your help." After handing his phone back to him, she stood and walked back toward the same doorway she had entered to find Olin.

"Get what you needed, Rebecca?" asked Feather.

"Olin was very helpful and appears to be a stelar employee."

"I agree. Don't know what I'd do without him."

Chapter 10

The Alias

Rebecca left Lumberjacks and immediately called Kenny. After four agonizing rings, he picked up.

"Good morning, Rebecca. I miss you too."

"Yes, I miss you. Kenny, remember those photos I collected for you?"

"Of course. We're still contacting people for follow-up interviews and questioning. Why?"

"I missed one. First, Marilyn Monroe wasn't Marilyn Monroe, she was Madonna from the Material Girl music video. She's wearing long pink gloves in that video. I couldn't see them in that picture because the waitress was blocking them."

"Just wearing gloves isn't a nail in the coffin. What else do you have?"

When Rebecca finished going over the details she had collected and put together from talking to Kathy and Olin, she had Kenny convinced she was right.

Once Olin said her name, everything fit. A small

town was nothing else if it wasn't a rumor mill. Things were said behind closed doors that somehow seemed to find their way to the ears of the general public and, occasionally, the local newspaper. It seemed only fitting that Ms. Hedgecomb was a hairdresser who had a shop on the same street as the library. It wasn't the salon Rebecca typically frequented, but she was going to try for a walk-in appointment today.

The tinkling of the bell as she opened the door was alarming because Rebecca was anxious about starting the conversation.

"Mornin'. How can we help you?" asked a full-figured woman standing at an empty station.

"I don't have an appointment, but I was just looking to get my split ends trimmed. I'm growing out my hair, so I don't want a full haircut. Is that possible?"

"Sure can. Name's Belinda. Why don't you have a seat?"

"Do you not have any appointment right now?" Rebecca looked around in a panic. She didn't see Ms. Hedgecomb anywhere though she swore she worked in this salon.

"I am free for another hour, and trimming up some split ends won't take that long, darlin'."

"Belinda hasn't had a full schedule this whole month, so you're good." A woman with jet black hair to her waist sashayed out from behind a curtain. She looked to be in her early sixties if Rebecca was guessing, and her hair could compete with Cher from the seventies.

"Hey, I just moved here. Don't listen to her. She's just

worried I'll steal her clients because she doesn't work a full schedule anymore."

"Oh, why is that?" Rebecca asked the woman who had just entered. "Ms. Hedgecomb, right?"

"That is right. I'm the owner, and I decided I'm ready to start slowing down in my old age. I'm taking fewer clients and renting out stations more often so I'll be ready to fully retire in the next year or two."

Rebecca sat in the chair on the left side of the salon while Ms. Hedgecomb was preparing some type of hair color for a woman in the chair on the right wall. She watched the salon through the mirror in front of her while Belinda got ready.

"Retiring sounds nice. What are your plans for when you retire?"

"I want to get a place down south somewhere so I don't have to shovel snow anymore. When my dear Leonard passed away, I had to pick up that chore, and I'm not fond of it."

"I'm sorry to hear about Leonard. How did he pass?" Rebecca knew Leonard had passed away, as did the entirety of Newfound Lake, and everyone had their suspicions.

"Fell down our stairs. He'd been taking a new medication that sometimes made him dizzy. The medical examiner said he had a high level of it in his system when he fell. It was tragic, but it will afford me the ability to retire sooner. I'd still rather have Leonard here, rest his soul, but it was a gift he couldn't give me otherwise."

Belinda got to work on Rebecca's hair. She crossed

her fingers and toes that there would be no mention of the lack of split ends and Belinda would happily accept the paying client in her chair regardless of the actual need.

"Wasn't Leonard's last name Dye? Weren't you Mrs. Wanda Dye when you named this place Curl Up & Dye? I've never heard a more perfect coincidence." Rebecca was working the room to get to the punchline.

"You've got me. Leonard was my second husband, so I wanted to go back to the same last name as my son."

"Your adult son, Jared?"

"That's right. With Leonard gone, I wanted us to have the same last name again. Jared Hedgecomb is the manager of the marina over by Wellington State Park."

"Ms. Hedgecomb, did I see you at the New Year's Eve party at The Glacial Inn?" Rebecca skipped right to the good part. She knew that the name Wanda Hedgecomb wasn't on the reservation list, and she wondered if she would deny attending since she went to such lengths to conceal her appearance. Was Rebecca's hunch a good one?

"What makes you think you saw me there?" She had been chatting while applying the color to her client's hair, but she turned to look in Rebecca's mirror when she was asked about attending the party.

"Well, I could have sworn there was a woman there dressed as Marilyn Monroe until I got to look at some of the pictures taken by other people who attended and posted to social media. I was quickly corrected by one who informed me the eighties icon in the hot pink dress was actually Madonna. With a blonde wig, that woman could have easily been you."

Before she could answer, another hair stylist chimed in. "Of course that was her. I made the reservations when she brought it up, and I went as Baby from Dirty Dancing. Did you see me in the photos? I carried a watermelon."

Wanda was now expected to respond. "I was there as Madonna. The waitress wanted a picture with me because we were both the Queen of Pop. The waiter was equally impressed. Why does my attendance matter?"

The tinkling of the bell to notify when the door had been opened rang again. Chief Towne entered and waited for the door to close behind him. "Ms. Hedgecome, my officer outside and I would like for you to join us at the station to answer some questions."

She looked around the salon, catching the eye of everyone else as they stared at her. "Why would you need me to come in for questioning? What have I done?"

"Are you the mother to Jared Hedgecomb?" Kenny asked.

"Of course. We were just talking about my son."

"Did your son recently finalize his divorce from Andrea Devine?"

She coughed and cleared her throat. With no options, she responded, "Yes. Little gold digger."

Rebecca asked, "Why would you say that? She's a server at Jilly's, right? I mean, it's not like she's rich."

"She's not rich yet. She took my Jared to court for a ridiculous alimony settlement. With the divorce finalized, he had to start payments on the first of January. I wasn't about to let her take everything he worked so hard for from him."

"How were you going to prevent it?" Rebecca had turned around in her chair and was looking directly at Wanda now.

"I know what you're thinking, and I'm not saying anything until I speak to my lawyer."

"Ms. Hedgecomb, you have every right to do that. Please come with me, and we'll read you your rights."

"Can I finish the job I'm in the middle of?"

"I'm sorry, but no. One of your co-workers will need to finish that for you."

She looked around. "Belinda?"

"Of course. Rebecca, can you wait so I can finish her color?"

"Not a problem. I completely understand." Rebecca smiled and nodded.

Kenny stepped forward. "Do I need to use the hand-cuffs, or will you come peacefully."

"I'll come with you since I haven't done anything."

With an additional officer outside the salon, Kenny escorted Ms. Hedgecomb to the back of the cruiser and drove off without any additional fanfare. Rebecca sat patiently and waited for the remainder of her trim while Belinda finished the color Wanda had started. No one said a single word for the thirty minutes Rebecca sat and waited. She paid a nominal fee and left a good tip for Belinda before heading home for the remainder of her day off.

* * *

When Rebecca started thinking about dinner, she felt her phone vibrate. A text message had come in from Kenny.

Kenny: Want me to bring pizza and fried pickles for dinner?

Rebecca: Sounds great.

Rebecca: Can I pick the movie?

Kenny: Cue it up for eight.

Kenny: See you then. XOXO

Rebecca smiled at the XOXO. It felt to her like they were still moving forward in their relationship emotionally. She knew she was in love with him, but they hadn't started saying it back and forth. The XOXO seemed like a step in that direction.

When the clock passed eight and Dirty Dancing was all cued up, she wondered where Kenny was. As a police officer, he had a reputation for punctuality. At half past eight she became worried. When she picked up her phone to send a text, headlights flooded the living room.

Rebecca opened the door as Kenny approached holding a pizza box, extra containers on top and an additional bag over his arm. He kicked off his boots at the door and entered with a kiss.

"Sorry, but we're gonna need to heat this up," he apologized. "I witnessed a car accident on the way here but after I had already picked up the food. I didn't have the time to send a message once I saw it. There was an ambulance that needed to be called, and statements, and..."

Rebecca interrupted, "Let's take this into the kitchen and talk about it." She took the food out of his hands.

"Is it okay if I get changed?"

"You don't need to ask permission to get changed here. I'll see you in the kitchen when you're ready."

Ten minutes later, the pizza was warm in the oven with the fried pickles. She had poured drinks for them and set the plates and silverware at their stools. Kenny sat in his spot. Rebecca served the mushroom pizza onto their plates and put a dish of fried pickles and ranch dressing between them.

"I'm not going to say that it wasn't frustrating and unnerving for you to be late. I'm not angry because I do understand it's part of your job, but I can see why Heather had a hard time with it."

Kenny's face showed the mention of Heather's name had hit him hard. "Should I be concerned you are ending what we have?"

"Absolutely not. We're two adults who need to share their feelings and concerns so the other has an opportunity to respond." Rebecca started to eat and waited for Kenny's response.

"It is part of the job, and it is not uncommon to be unable to even send a message. Do you have any idea how we can proceed to make this easier for you?"

"While I was worried about you, I started to Google solutions. Trying not to assume the worst, I found a handheld GPS system that hikers use."

He scrunched his eyebrows together. "Go on."

"Well, you could clip it to your work belt. It lets you

program in a few short messages and a number to send them to. You could program a late message, an emergency message and a message to let me know everything is okay. I'm not looking for reinforcement when you're working on a regular basis, just if we have plans that are being impacted. Do you think that could work?"

"I can do that. Did you find some options you can share with me?"

"We can do that later. Let's eat and watch the movie."

Kenny picked up his plate, drink and silverware. "Let's eat in the living room, if that's okay with you."

"That works for me." She picked up her food and followed. "Hey, did she confess? If you can tell me, that is. Please know that I can take it if the answer is no." They sat on opposite couches and lowered their items to the central coffee table.

"The off-the-record answer is that she did confess, and you were completely correct about the gloves. We still don't know where the black glove came from, and we may never know. With the confession, it goes into an evidence locker just in case it matters, but it probably won't. I was shocked that she made the shot. She said she fired from the hip so people wouldn't see the gun, and it worked! One of those improbable but possible instances I'll never see again in my career."

"Never say never," she warned. "Wait. You said you searched everyone as they left. Wouldn't that include her purse or wherever she was keeping the gun?"

"We did, and she had nothing on her. Turns out, she

dropped the gun down an air vent in the floor before she left. They have an updated system in the building now, but it was going to be costly to remove the old one. Instead, they just disconnected it but left the vents in the floor. She saw an opportunity to cover her tracks, and she took it."

Rebecca lifted the remote, and before pressing play she asked Kenny, "Do you want to spend the night in these arms of mine?"

"Because you're some kind of wonderful, I'd like to stay."

Also by Virginia K. Bennett

A Newfound Lake Cozy Mystery:

Catch of the Day

A View From The Ledge

Once Inn A Lifetime

Potluck of the Draw

With Sugar on Roundtop

Err on the Side Dish of Caution

Hand Caught in the Christmas Cookie Jar

* * *

The Mysteries of Cozy Cove:

Much Ado About Muffin

It's All or Muffin

Muffin to Lose

Nothing Ventured, Muffin Gained

You Ain't Seen Muffin Yet

Here Goes Muffin

Recipe

Potato Crust Quiche
Ingredients:
2 cups frozen shredded hash browns (thawed)
1 cup milk
4 eggs
1/4 tsp pepper
4 oz shredded cheddar cheese
1 cup deli ham, cubed
Optional: Mushrooms, Peppers, Onions, Cooked Bacon

Preheat oven to 375 degrees.
Press potato in paper towels to remove as much moisture
as possible.
Spray 9-inch pie dish (ceramic) with non-stick cooking
spray. Press hash browns on bottom and sides of pie dish.
Bake until potatoes are golden and starting to get crisp.
Sprinkle 1/2 cup of cheese on the bottom of the potato
crust.

Combine milk, eggs and pepper. Beat well then stir in ham and 1/2 cup of cheese.

(Additional ingredients can be added at this time except mushrooms.)

Pour mixture over the cheese and potato crust. Add mushroom slices on top at this time if desired.

Bake 35-40 minutes. Let stand 10 minutes before cutting.

(If you add mushrooms, the top will be wet. Use paper towels to soak up excess moisture.)

About the Author

When she's not writing on her couch with her two cats, Twyla and Geo, Virginia is busy teaching middle school math, grocery shopping, cooking or spending time with her husband and son. Together, her small family loves to go geocaching and visit theme parks.

Mysteries have always been an interesting challenge for Virginia, much like watching a magician perform. Unless you want to hear the entire thought process behind who she thinks is the killer and why, you might want to avoid watching any movies together.

The path to publishing a book is different for everyone and her path is full of twists and turns. Thank you to those who support the journey.

facebook.com/VirginiaKBennett

instagram.com/authorvkbennett

Made in the USA
Las Vegas, NV
05 January 2024